© First Edition: 30 September 1999
Designed by Catherine McIntyre
Published by K. Pohlmann
Printed by Akzent Printing & Grafix, Los Angeles, CA
Printed in Korea
ISBN: 1-890377-06-6

Pohlmann Press / Naked Gallery
7336 Santa Monica Boulevard, #714, Los Angeles, California 90046-6616
USA Tel/Fax: 323.782.1978
www.pohlmannpress.com

Catherine McIntyre was born in 1961, and lives in Scotland.
She has a degree in Illustration from
Duncan of Jordanstone College of Art, Dundee,
and a Masters degree in Photography from the same college.
She began making digital imagery in 1996;
this work has been published in many periodicals
around the world, and on several websites.
This is her first book.

for
Jac
1996 - 1999

Deliquescence

Catherine McIntyre

Foreword

I first met Catherine McIntyre on the Internet while searching for interesting and unusual photographs to view. What attracted me to her web site, in the jungle of available images on the Internet, was the tantalizing title of her work, 'Dreams and Nightmares'. Not knowing what to expect and not expecting what I found, my first reaction was one of amazement. The craftsmanship of her combinatory digital images was extraordinary. The images possessed their own aesthetic; they were seamless and did not look digitally composed. Once past this initial phase of looking, I found myself riveted to the images, fascinated by their content, puzzled and challenged by the latent meaning they held. In my email response to her images, I found that the author was a young lady from Dundee in Scotland.

In looking at her work from a historical perspective, one observes that McIntyre works in the style of earlier artists who used collage and montage, artists such as Picasso, Braque, Robinson, Rejlander, Heartfield, Barbara Morgan, and the contemporary artist, Jerry Uelsmann. What McIntyre does so brilliantly is to extend the work of integrated images using digital technology in such a way that it defies recognition of the medium used. She takes full advantage of its versatility, and has mastered it, which allows her easily to combine and layer images from a wide variety of sources, change scale, change colors, sharpen, soften, add or remove texture, and so on; and, when necessary, change the changes.

The central figure in her assemblies is the classical female nude which she meticulously surrounds with a variety of familiar visual and verbal signifiers from different times and different places, signifiers that suggest and invite numerous possible associations. Although the signifiers are recognizable and definable, the gestalt that takes form is beyond the verbal. Her completed assembly becomes an archetypal image, which serves to trigger events in our subliminal dream world. Dreams, as the aborigines of Australia believe, are shadows of something real. Catherine McIntyre's images cast such shadows. Her carefully layered, surreal images pose a challenge to viewers searching for meaning and closure. Although the content is recognizable, the meaning is not readily apparent and it must remain so. Baudelaire reminds us that 'To define is to destroy, to suggest is to create'. McIntyre's oeuvre of images suggest but do not define, they invite us to open our eyes, mind and heart in our relationships to each other, to nature and to times past, present and future. With the proposed opening of a digital art museum in New York and elsewhere, Catherine McIntyre's images may soon find a home. She is sure to become one of the recognized digital artists of the 21st Century.

Richard D. Zakia
Professor Emeritus
Rochester Institute of Technology
USA

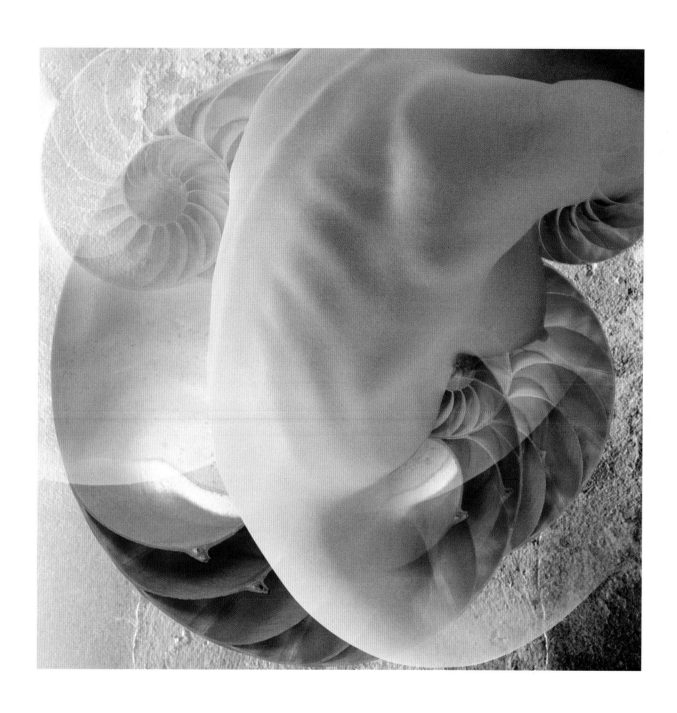

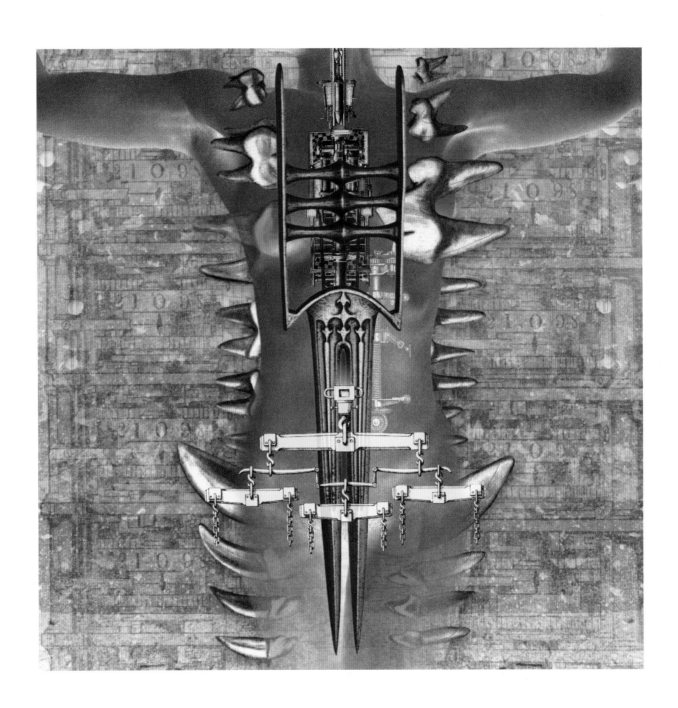

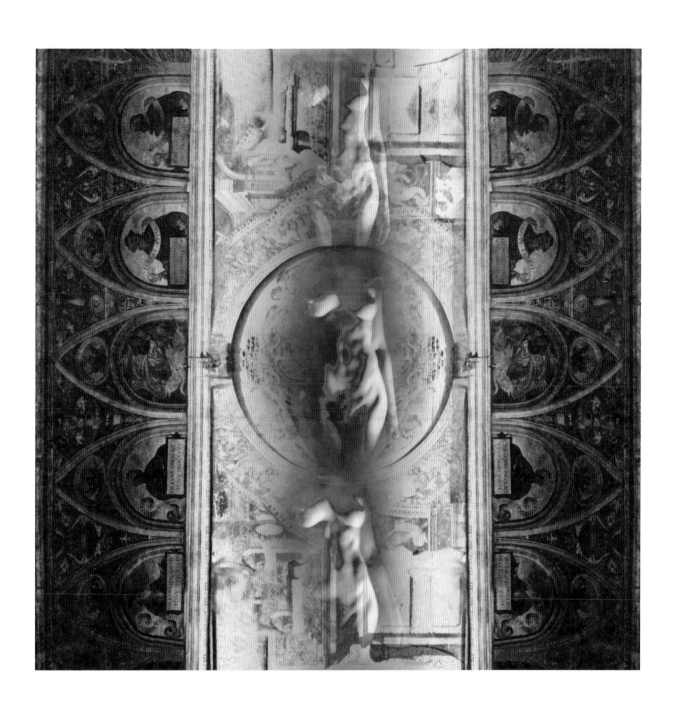

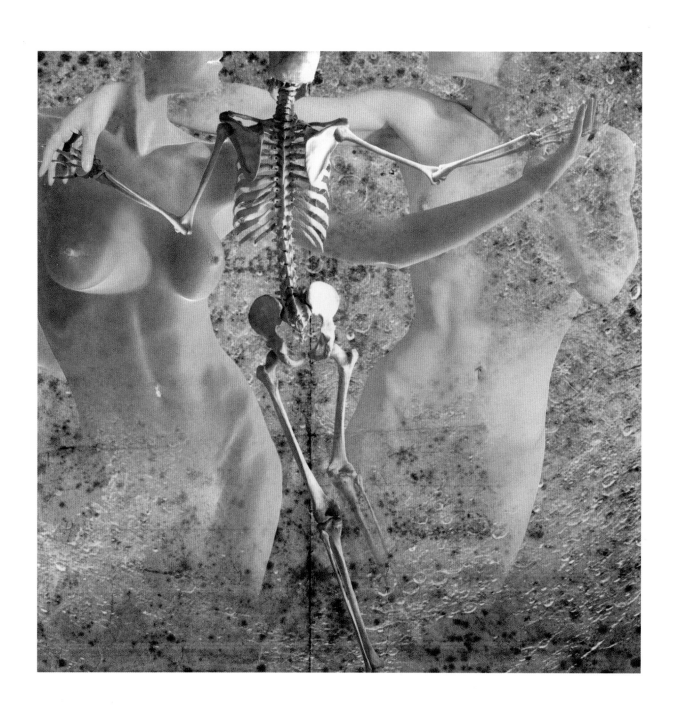

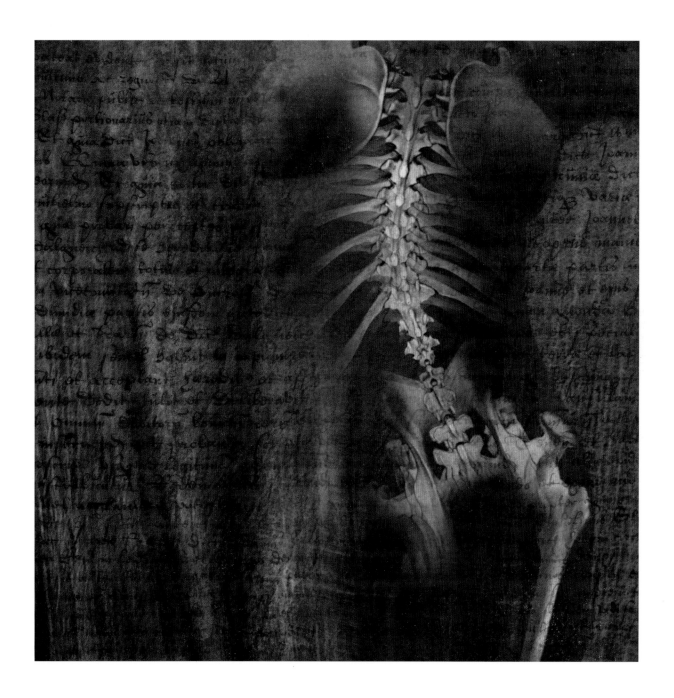

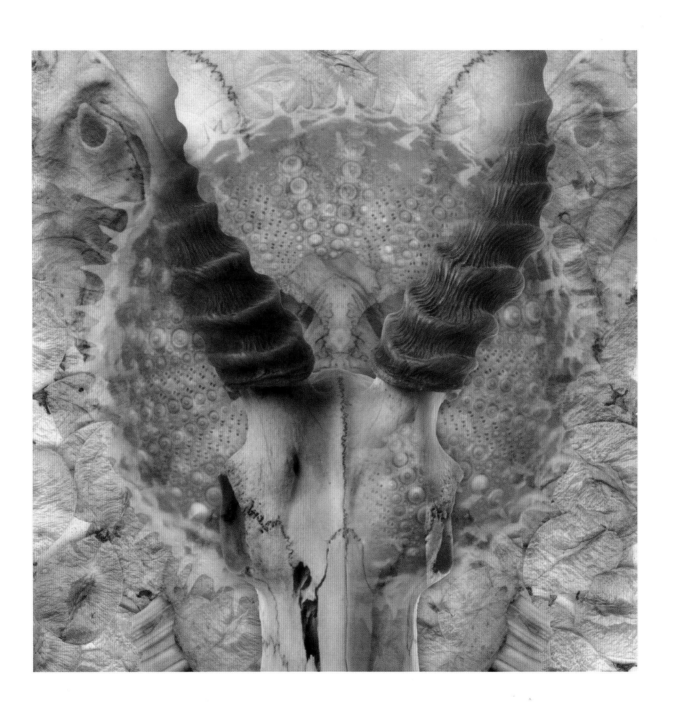

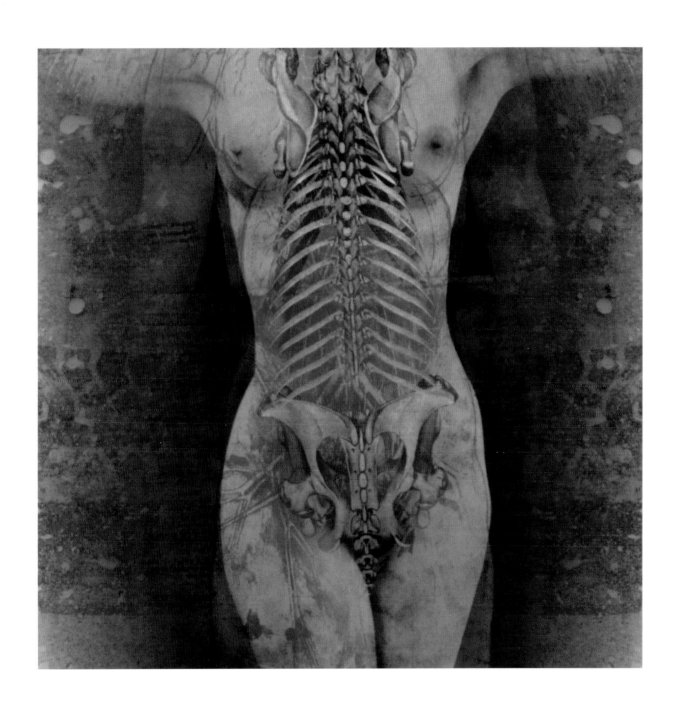

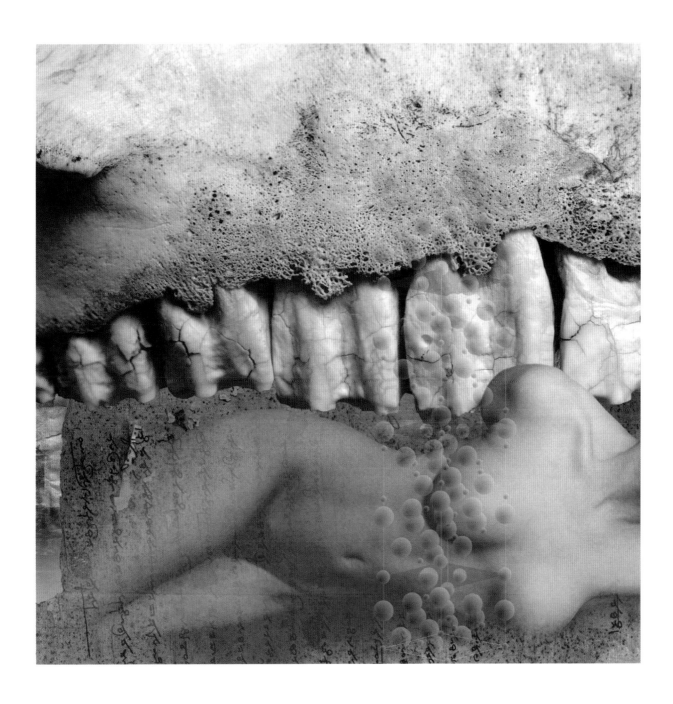

Une chose ne peut être
à deux places à la fois
On ne peut pas l'avoir en
tête et sous les yeux

Post card — Carte Postale

Mrs. Wright
The Sherwood Foresters
10 Ulsoor Road
Bangalore

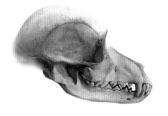

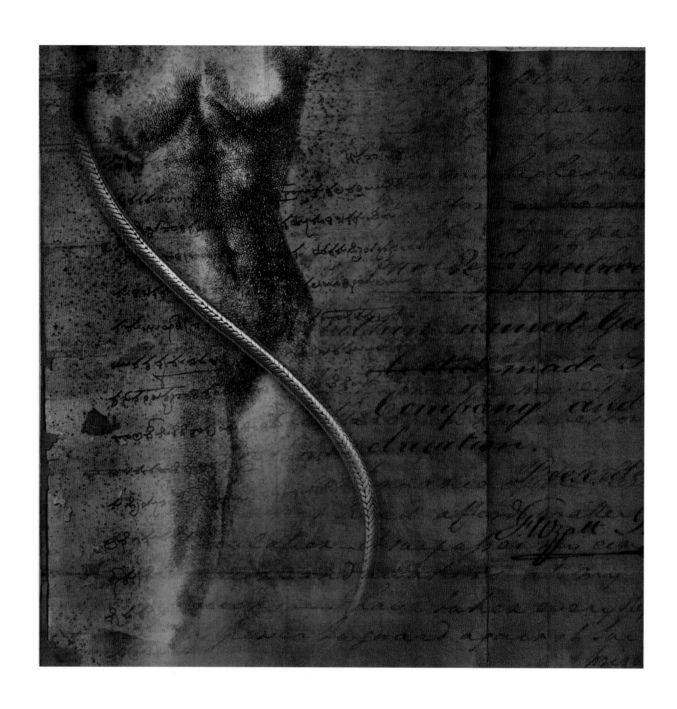

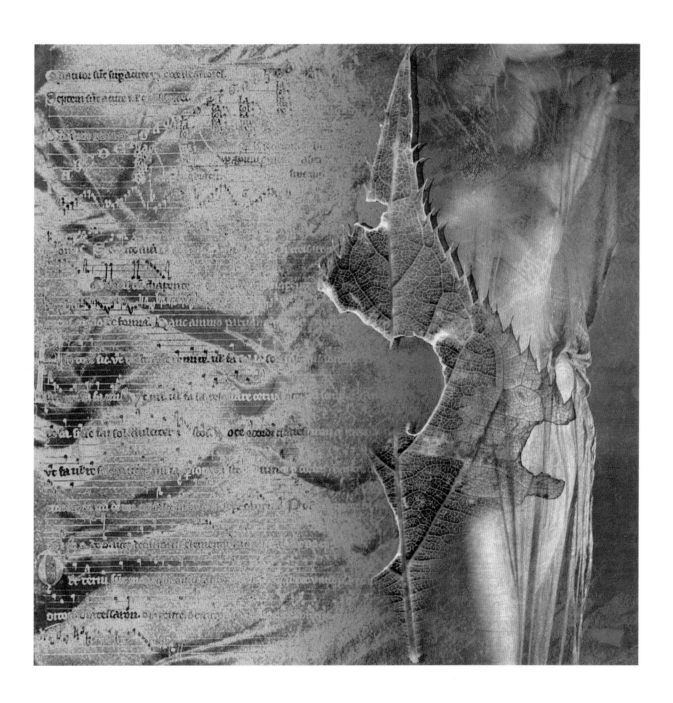

Contents

1   echoes

2   mechanoid

3   ascension

5   recessional

6   zebras

7   books

8   astrology

9   caught

11   cold is lonely

12   three graces

13   coralline

14   advancing

15   the act of not writing

16   stress fractures - for Renée

17   crocuses

18   crucifix

19   disparue

21   demon

22   the future

23   dialogue

25   divided

26   truthtelling

27   dreamscape

28   deerheads

29   organic

30   bad angel

31   insubstance

32   elegy

33   parchment

35   falling angel

36   spring

37   float

39   golden textbook

41   phoenix

42   anticipation

43   hopeward bound

44   victory

45   stretch

47   interior

48   weights and measures

49   biology

51   it looks still

53   long distance kiss

54   trapped

55   Piranesi's prison

57   mermaid

59   ministry of truth

60   the wait

61   mirrored

62   money talks

63   vellum

65   necromancer

66   scaled

67   passage of time

68   strong

69   pressure of time

71   spikes

73   rock pool

74   honesty

75   seraphim

76   creep

77   song

79   inner flight

81   astronomy

83   angel

The quotation on page 52 is from Georges Braque (1882-1963).

TECHNICAL INFORMATION

McIntyre works currently on a PowerMac 8600/250 in Photoshop 4.0. Original photographs were taken on a Nikon F401 (28-80mm zoom lens) usually at the 'macro' end of the lens - close up, the textures and lack of scale of abstract images, which are vital to the later work, take precedence over the subject. The nude elements are studio shots, made in collaboration with Sean Earnshaw of the University of St Andrews on a Bronica SQ 6x6 camera with an 80mm lens. The component parts of the images were scanned on a UMAX Astra 1200S flatbed scanner, a Nikon Coolscan or a Dainippon Screen colour drum scanner. Original material includes positive colour film, negative black and white film (Agfapan 100), drawings, collages or found objects.

MAKING A DIGITAL MONTAGE

All these images began life as a series of scans on a computer; Photoshop 4.0 is the programme that brings all the elements together. The standard collage techniques, used since Braque invented them, are all here. Any number of elements can be pasted into a picture, in layers one on top of another; the order in which they are placed can be changed at any time. The elements can be trimmed and rotated, just as with a paper montage. However, Photoshop allows much more. The scale of the various parts can be altered, and they can be distorted, for example to create a perspective effect. Then, opacity can be varied, either across an entire layer or in parts using a layer mask. Contrast, hue, and saturation are further variables. Each layer can also interact with the ones below it by using layer modes. The luminosity mode, for example, makes the layer it is applied to take on the hue of the layer below, while retaining its own tonal and contrast values.

ABOUT THE WORK

McIntyre is from an illustration background, currently working as a freelance artist.
The work presented here is the latest in an ongoing personal project which has been developing for many years, through a variety of media, along several major themes.

The nude is a natural symbol of the laying-bare of innermost feelings, and has been a continuing metaphor in the work. It can radiate well-being, or vulnerability and weakness; it can symbolize humanity's deepest essence, or that of the natural world; it can be idealized, realistic, grotesque, dismembered, impersonal, abstracted. The endless ways of representing the nude all carry with them resonances inevitably associated with the depiction of ourselves at our most unprotected. Images of the nude are impossible to ignore.

She began in the life studio, which teaches an understanding of form, light, and dimension. An abiding fascination with anatomy, the mechanics and moods of the body, and measurement was born here. A Masters degree in photography began the exploration of a nude at once more, and less, literal than that of the drawing class. The images began to assert themselves, to become ends in themselves; they learned to express very personal philosophies, obsessions, states of mind and emotions.

The layering techniques available in Photoshop were a revelation. Initial attempts at collage had always been restricted by the given scale and colour of found objects and photographs, and by the physical problems of attachment; translucency, too, was not a variable. In Photoshop, there are no such restrictions. Images can be compiled from widely differing sources and fine-tuned with unprecedented subtlety into a coherent whole.

The images are intended to work on two levels. On the aesthetic level of texture, colour and pattern, the work is often about finding correlations between natural and manufactured objects in decay. The laws of physics act equally upon nature and the work of man; some pictures show nature asserting itself and reducing man's efforts to their original elements, while others have nature under threat from encroaching industrialization. This latter feeling of weight, crushing, compaction, pinning down and hemming in, isolation and ultimately of threat, became elements of the second, emotional level of the work.

The theme of aging is therefore important in the textural elements of the work; the beautiful effects of weathering and distressing on often very unprepossessing substrates being at once destructive and creative carries a paradox mirrored in the aging of the individual.

A second major theme is the difficulties of communication. Any conversation is a microcosm of the dissembling, misunderstanding and pretense of everyday transactions. The space between implication and inference, into which so much of importance seems to disappear, the gap between the projected and the true self, the misapprehensions inevitable when thoughts are translated, more or less efficiently, or not at all, into words - all these are the subject of much of her latest work. The nude has become a symbol of veracity, lack of pretense, honesty - and vulnerability.

My sincere thanks go to:

Mr Sean Earnshaw, for his collaboration in making the nude elements of these pictures,
and without whose talent, imagination, patience and hard work
this project would have been impossible

Dr Richard Zakia, for his Foreword, and for his continuing insight and encouragement

My parents, for support, advice and both nature and nurture

Mr Charles Craig, for lending his expert eye

Mr Jonathan Robertson and Mr Sandy Tulloch, for sowing the seeds

Mrs Margaret Smith and Mrs Rhona Rutherford, for drum scanning and eclectic collecting

Mr Dave Roche and Mr Jim Allen, for technical assistance

Mr David 'Chunks' Chambers, for early guidance

Dr Colin Affleck and Mr Naasan, for content!

Jac, Lugs and Berry, for inspiration and friendship

and Alistair, for so much.

Thank you, Klaus Gerhart, for making this happen!